THE GRUMPY PETS

Kristine A. Lombardi

Abrams Books for Young Readers
New York

Library of Congress Cataloging-in-Publication Data

Lombardi, Kristine A., author, illustrator.
The grumpy pets / by Kristine A. Lombardi.
pages cm
Summary: "Billy is a grumpy boy who's not like the other kids. His mother takes him and his
sister, Sara, to the animal shelter one Saturday in hope of cheering him up. But the pets he
sees are too happy for his taste. Then he finds the grumpy pets. . ."—Provided by publisher.
ISBN 978-1-4197-1888-5
[1. Pets—Fiction.] I. Title.
PZ7.L83316Gr 2016
[E]—dc23
2015016388

Text and illustrations copyright © 2016 Kristine A. Lombardi
Book design by Pamela Notarantonio

Printed and bound in China
10 9 8 7 6 5 4 3 2 1

Abrams Books for Young Readers are available at special discounts when purchased
in quantity for premiums and promotions as well as fundraising or educational use.
Special editions can also be created to specification. For details, contact
specialsales@abramsbooks.com or the address below.

ABRAMS
THE ART OF BOOKS SINCE 1949
115 West 18th Street
New York, NY 10011
www.abramsbooks.com

To Miss Freckles—the grumpiest (albeit most adored) pet of all time, 1992-2011

And to Boo—my sweet rescue cat who really rescued me

Mom took Billy and Sara to
Perfect Pets one Saturday.

Mom worried that Billy always seemed unhappy.

She hoped that a special trip would give him a reason to smile.

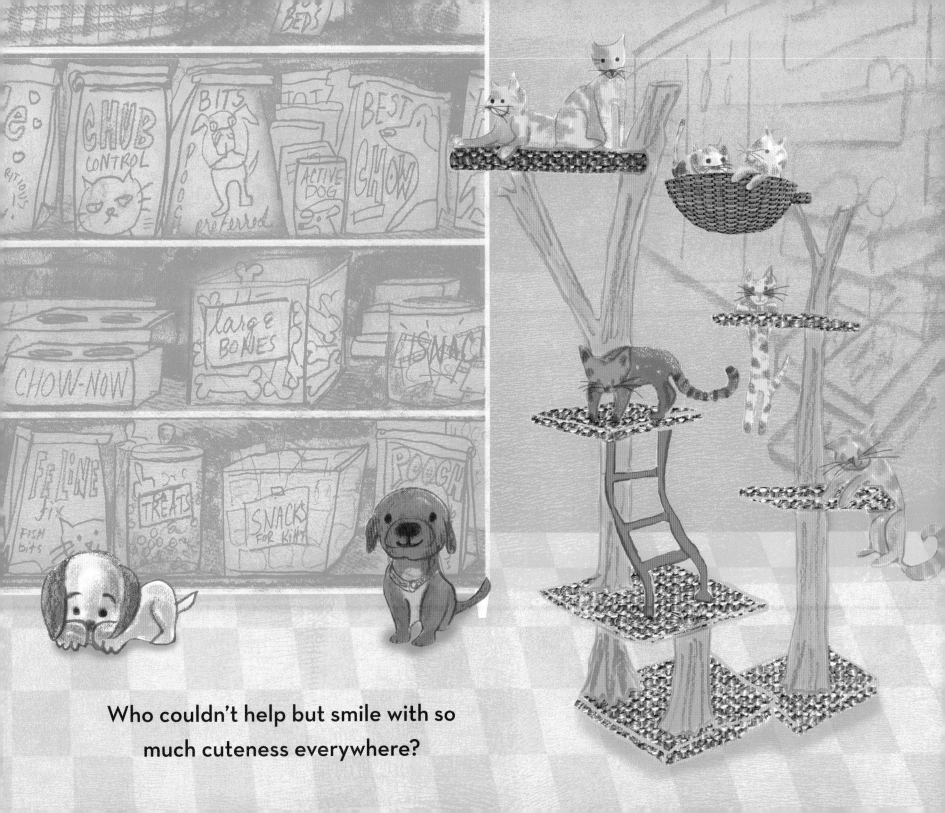

Who couldn't help but smile with so
much cuteness everywhere?

It seemed everyone was finding their perfect pets.

Especially Sara.

But Billy was not amused.

He began to look around,

but every single pet was just so *happy.*

Blech, Billy thought to himself.

So he walked up and down the aisles. Then he heard a noise.

And there, in the back, were . . .

Row upon row

of scruffy,

grouchy faces.

They were crabby, cranky, and moody.

A little like . . . Billy.

Billy stared at one of the dogs.

And the dog
stared right back.

Billy made
a face.

So did the dog.

Billy took a
step closer.

The dog did, too.

And then . . .

slurp!

The volunteer handed Billy the dog.

And then Billy
held him.

They stayed like that
for a long time.

Everyone had found their perfect pet.

Even Billy.